The Hint in the
Peeping Pupil

**Written & Illustrated
by Ken Bowser**

Solving Mysteries Through
Science, Technology, Engineering, Art & Math

**RED
CHAIR
·PRESS·**

Egremont, Massachusetts

The Jesse Steam Mysteries are produced and published by:

Red Chair Press LLC   PO Box 333   South Egremont, MA 01258-0333

www.redchairpress.com

 FREE Educator Guide at www.redchairpress.com/free-resources

For My Grandson, Liam

Publisher's Cataloging-In-Publication Data

Names: Bowser, Ken, author, illustrator.
Title: The hint in the peeping pupil / written & illustrated by Ken Bowser.
Other Titles: Peeping pupil

Description: South Egremont, MA : Red Chair Press, [2021] | Series: A
    Jesse Steam mystery | "Solving Mysteries Through Science, Technology,
    Engineering, Art & Math." | Includes a word list and hands-on
    Makerspace activity. | Interest age level: 008-011. | Summary: "When
    Jesse stops by The Curiosity Shop, her favorite place to snoop around,
    she uncovers an old painting in a dusty, antique steamer trunk. But
    what happens later that night when Jesse is startled by a creepy
    eyeball? Find out how Professor Peach helps her use the skills of an
    artist to uncover the mystery of The Hint in the Peeping Pupil"—
    Provided by publisher.

Identifiers: ISBN 9781643710181 (library hardcover) | ISBN 9781643710198
    (paperback) | ISBN 9781643710204 (ebook)

Subjects: LCSH: Painting--Conservation and restoration--Juvenile fiction.
    | Eye in art--Juvenile fiction. | Research--Juvenile fiction. | CYAC:
    Painting--Conservation and restoration--Fiction. | Eye in art--Fiction.
    | Research--Fiction. | LCGFT: Detective and mystery fiction.

Classification: LCC PZ7.B697 Hi 2021 (print) | LCC PZ7.B697 (ebook) | DDC
    [Fic]--dc23

LC record available at https://lccn.loc.gov/2020934646

Printed in the United States of America

0920 1P CGS21

Table of Contents

Cast of Characters
Meet Jesse, Mr. Stubbs & The Gang   4

Town Map
Find Your Way Around Deanville   6

Chapter 1
Seek and You Shall Find   8

Chapter 2
Curiosity Thrilled the Cat 14

Chapter 3
A Musty Trunk and a Hidden Treasure 20

Chapter 4
Paws for Thought 26

Chapter 5
Jeepers Creepers, What are Those Crazy Peepers? 32

Chapter 6
Temporary Tempera or The Foil of the Oil 38

Chapter 7
Birds in the Boneyard 48

Chapter 8
A Brazen Raven and a Grave Discovery 54

Jesse's Word List 62

Makerspace Activity: Try It Out! 64

Cast of Characters

Jesse Steam

Amateur sleuth and all-around neat kid. Jesse loves riding her bike, solving mysteries, and most of all, Mr. Stubbs. Jesse is never without her messenger bag and the cool stuff it holds.

Mr. Stubbs

A cat with an attitude, he's the coolest tabby cat in Deanville. Stubbs was a stray cat who strayed right into Jesse's heart. Can you figure out how he got his name?

Professor Peach

A retired university professor. Professor Peach knows tons of cool stuff and is somewhat of a legend in Deanville. He has college degrees in Science, Technology, Engineering, Art, and Math.

Emmett

Professor Peach's ever-present pet, white lab rat. He loves cheese balls, and wherever you find The Professor, you're sure to find Emmett—even though he might be difficult to spot!

Clark & Lewis

Jesse's next-door neighbor and sometimes formidable adversary, Clark Johnson, and his slippery, slimy, gross-looking pet frog, Lewis. Yuck.

Dorky Dougy

Clark Johnson's three-year-old, tag-along baby brother. Dougy is never without his stuffed alligator, a rubber knife, and something really goofy to say, like "eleventy-seven."

Kimmy Kat Black

Holder of the Deanville Elementary School Long Jump Record, know-it-all, and self-proclaimed future member of Mensa. Kimmy Kat Black lives near the Spooky Tree.

Liam LePoole

A black belt in karate and also the captain of the Deanville Community Swimming Pool Cannonball Team. Liam's best friend is Chompy Dog, his stinky, gassy, and frenzied, brown puggle.

Mr. Winkle

Constant companion to Mr. Flarity. Mr. Winkle loves to collect fine china and enjoys 18th century poetry and classical music.

Mr. Flarity

Mr. Flarity lives with Mr. Winkle above The Curiosity Shop with their cat, Cali. He loves quiet evenings at home and long walks on the beach.

The Town of Deanville

Seek and You Shall Find

Chapter 1

"Where is that blasted thing?" Jesse said to Mr. Stubbs as she dug frantically through her dresser drawer. "It has to be around here somewhere! I saw it five minutes ago! I can't start my day without it," she complained.

Jesse carried on digging through her dresser drawer. "Well. There's that stupid yo-yo I misplaced a year ago. That's not it." Jesse threw the yo-yo over her shoulder and kept on with her frenzied digging.

Out flew a year-old, half-eaten sandwich. "Gross. That's not it." She cringed. Next came her long-lost, left flip-flop. "Stupid flip-flop!" A hairbrush. A hairy wad of silly putty. A mostly empty box of crayons. A doll's head. A leaky squirt gun. And a kazoo.

"But where is my dang magnifying glass?" Jesse groaned.

Jesse turned her attention to the clothes hamper that was in the back corner of her bedroom. "Maybe it ended up in here," she mumbled to herself as she flung dirty socks and underwear and t-shirts in every direction. "NOTHING!" she screeched.

Giving up, Jesse plopped down on the floor. "I just don't feel complete if I don't have my magnifying glass with me in my messenger bag. Ya never know when you might need it to solve a mystery," she said to Stubbs as he stood to stretch.

"Stubbs! What am I going to do with you? You were sitting on top of it all this time!" Jesse yelled at Stubbs.

With a twitch of his tail, Stubbs jumped down from his perch on the bed revealing the once hidden magnifying glass. "C'mon, you wacky cat. Let's head to the park. I'll clean this mess up later." And with that, Jesse and Stubbs headed outside.

CAN YOU FIND THE HIDDEN OBJECTS?

THE TREEHOUSE · LEWIS · A SCYAMORE SEED · CHOMPY'S HOUSE · EMMETT

Stubbs assumed his normal position on the front of Jesse's bike as they rode through Deanville. "Isn't it crazy, Stubbs?" she asked.

"All of the things that you never even notice if you don't bother to look close enough."

A CROOKED CRAYON · AN ACORN · A BAT · A FLASHLIGHT · A BLUEBIRD

13.

Curiosity Thrilled the Cat

Chapter 2

Leaving their house on her bike, Jesse and Mr. Stubbs crossed over The Creepy Bridge. They turned left past The Thinkin' Tree and pedaled up to The Curiosity Shop.

"It's been a while since we've visited Mr. Flarity and Mr. Winkle," Jesse told Stubbs, and she hopped off her bike. "Let's see what cool stuff they have in here today."

Jesse twisted the old, metal doorknob to the shop door and pushed it opened with a long, slow "creeeeak." The bell at the top of the door clanged, and the OPEN sign slapped the glass window as Jesse pulled the door shut behind them with a clang and a slap.

The Curiosity Shop was a peculiar place. The items that Mr. Flarity and Mr. Winkle filled it with were even more peculiar still.

"In the market for a real shrunken head?"

Jesse asked Stubbs. Jesse held the freaky
thing up by its hair and dangled it in front
of Mr. Stubbs' nose. "Gaa-ross!" she said as
she dropped the shriveled head back down
on the countertop. Jesse walked by an eerie
looking, coin-operated fortune teller, its
glassy eyes following her as she passed.
"That thing gives me the creeps," she said
to Stubbs. At the back of the dark shop, an

ancient mummy peered down at Jesse and Stubbs from behind a tall shelf that held too many oddities to count.

"Genuine Wooden Pirate's Hook," Jesse read the sign on the counter in front of a brown, handless arm. "I bet it would be hard to tie your shoes in the morning wearing this thing," she chuckled to Mr. Stubbs.

Jesse lifted a heavy, rock-like thing and read the card that was attached. "A fossilized Mastodon tooth," she read the tag out loud. "What in the world is a Mastodon?"

Row after row, shelf after shelf, The Curiosity Shop was jammed packed with the bizarre oddities that Mr. Winkle and Mr. Flarity had gathered, one by one, from all corners of the globe.

"Check this out, Stubby, old boy. A fossil of a prehistoric Cryptolithus Trilobite. Whatever that is." She studied the odd-looking rock through her magnifying glass.

"And here's something you don't see every day. A traditional Dogon ceremonial mask." Jesse held the hairy, scary looking mask up to her face and looked over at her reflection in a tall, dusty old mirror. "Yikes! I'd hate to run into this guy in a dark alley."

Jesse turned back to the counter and began to sort through a bowl of big, shiny marbles. But suddenly, Jesse noticed something very strange. The marbles were starring back. "ARRRRGH!" Jesse screamed to Stubbs, "It's a bowl of glass eyeballs!"

A Musty Trunk and a Hidden Treasure

Chapter 3

Still in shock from the glass eyeballs, Jesse backed away from the glaring bowl of creepy peepers. "Well, that's enough to send a shiver up your spine," she said to the cat who was still cowering in the corner.

As Jesse stepped further back, she found herself sitting on the top of a large, musty, old steamer trunk that had been pushed back into the corner of the dark Curiosity Shop. The trunk's heavy, brass lock and latches rattled as Jesse sat, and she felt the thick leather straps that buckled the trunk shut. There were big wooden handles on either side of the trunk that were used to lift it.

Colorful, aged travel stickers, depicting exotic destinations from all around the world, covered the old trunk. Along with one set of gold initials. "P.O.D." the initials read.

"I love this old trunk," Jesse said to Stubbs. "Can you imagine the stories this musty, old thing could tell?"

"Foreign lands. Romantic ports of call. Tropical full moons and balmy breezes. I wonder what's inside."

Jesse unbuckled the straps, lifted the shiny, brass latches, and raised the heavy lid on the musty, old steamer trunk. "Aww. It's empty," she said to Stubbs with a disappointed sigh. With that, Stubbs jumped in and began clawing at the bottom of the old trunk. "What are you doing, you crazy feline?"

As Stubbs clawed away, Jesse could see something below the bottom of the trunk. "Hey, Stubbs. You're on to something here. This trunk has a secret compartment!"

Jesse lifted the false bottom of the old steamer trunk and revealed something remarkable. "It's an old painting, Stubbs!

An old painting of flowers!" Jesse pulled
the painting from the trunk and dusted
it off with her bandanna. Its gilded frame
presented a beautiful, old patina. "This is
beautiful," she whispered to Stubbs.

"Well, hello Jesse. What have you found
there?" Two familiar voices broke Jesse's
concentration on the old painting.

"Mr. Flarity! Mr. Winkle! Oh, hi! I found
this cool painting hidden in the bottom of

this old steamer trunk. It's of hydrangea flowers," she said to the couple as she turned the painting toward them. "My favorite!"

"My. It is lovely. Isn't it, Mr. Flarity?" Mr. Winkle said.

"Well, yes it is, Mr. Winkle," Mr. Flarity returned.

"Why don't you just take it home with you Jesse, my dear," the two replied. "I believe you'll give it a good home."

Chapter 4

Jesse balanced the old painting in the basket on the front of her bike, behind Mr. Stubbs, and headed home.

"Hey Jesse!" A familiar voice called out. "What's that on the front of your bike?"

Jesse stopped to see Kimmy Kat Black swinging from the tire swing that hung from The Thinkin' Tree.

"This? It's a painting of some hydrangea flowers that I found in an old trunk at The Curiosity Shop. Aren't they beautiful?" she went on to Kimmy Kat Black. "Mr. Flarity and Mr. Winkle said I could have it."

"Ah! Hydrangea macrophylla," Kimmy Kat Black exclaimed. "A species of flowering plant in the family Hydrangeaceae, native to Japan," she boasted. Kimmy Kat Black was always boasting about something. "As a

future member of Mensa," she blathered on, "I try to keep up with things of a botanical nature," Kimmy Kat Black said with a smirk.

Jesse held the painting up so that Kimmy could see it better. "Don't you just love it?" Jesse asked. Then, without a bit of warning, Mr. Stubbs leapt from his place in the basket and began chasing after a yellow butterfly. The butterfly went flying. Stubbs went flying, and the painting went flying to the ground.

"Stuuuuuubbs! You crazy cat!" Jesse yelled.

Jesse and Kimmy Kat Black laughed while Stubbs batted at the butterfly as it fluttered away. "Now look what you've done silly," Jesse scolded Mr. Stubbs with a smile. "It looks like, thanks to you,

we have a little extra cleaning to do when we get this home."

When Jesse and Stubbs got back into her room that afternoon, she set the painting down on her desk.

"Well, it doesn't look like it was damaged by your shenanigans in any way, Stubby, old boy," she said to the cat as she surveyed the canvas.

"Just a big, muddy paw print." Jesse wiped the paw print off of the painting with her bandanna and a bit of water and set it back down on her desk. "There. Now see if you can stay off it for a while, you flaky feline."

Jeepers Creepers, What are Those Crazy Peepers?

Chapter 5

With Mr. Stubbs looking on, Jesse straightened up her room and got ready for bed while reflecting on her day.

"Hey, remember that creepy Dogon ceremonial mask we saw at The Curiosity Shop today, Stubby? That thing was totally disturbing," she said as she packed her stuff back into her messenger bag.

"The shrunken head was super freaky too. And those eerie glass eyeballs! Can you believe those things? I hope they don't find their way into my dreams tonight."

She lifted the painting and held it up on either side by its frame.

"This is a good spot, don't you think?" she remarked to Stubbs, who was now fast asleep. Jesse hung the painting on the wall across from her bed.

The evening grew quiet. The birds stopped chirping, and the moon came out to cast a beautiful, blue light through Jesse's window.

"Good night, Stubby," she whispered. Stubbs purred softly.

It wasn't long before Jesse and Stubbs were both sound asleep. Thankfully, none of the creepy things from The Curiosity Shop interrupted her snoozing. But something did!

Sca-raaaatch! Sca-raaaatch! Sca-raaaaaaaaatch!

"What was that!?" Jesse sprang up in her bed, jarred from her deep slumber.

Scratch!

She heard it again. "Stubbs? Is that you making that scratching noise? I hope." Stubbs was right next to her in bed cowering under the sheets. Turning back toward the noise, Jesse noticed the branch that was scrapping against her bedroom window.

"Oh. It was just the wind moving that
branch," she comforted Stubbs.

"Good night again, Mr. Stubbs." Jesse
rolled over to look at her cat. "What is wrong
with you now?" she said to Mr. Stubbs, who
was staring wide-eyed across the room as

if he had just seen a ghost. Jesse turned to see what had caught Stubbs' attention. And then she saw it. One big, creepy, illuminated eyeball was staring right back at them from across Jesse's dark, shadowy bedroom!

"Do... you... see... what... I... see?" Jesse questioned Stubbs in an anxious, shaking voice. "It's... it's... it's... it's an EYEBALL!"

Jesse yanked the covers up over her head only to slide them back down again slowly so only her eyes were peeking out from the top.

"Stubbs? Stubbs? What is that?" she whimpered nervously.

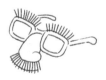

Temporary Tempera or the Foil of the Oil

Chapter 6

The frightened duo sat frozen and shaking under the sheets. They stared back from behind the blankets at the giant, terrifying eyeball.

Jesse thought and thought. Slowly, she began to make some sense of this strange situation.

"Stubbs," Jesse whispered almost silently. "That eyeball is coming from the hydrangea painting. And I think it's from right where I removed your muddy footprint."

Jesse mustered the courage to remove herself from the security of her blanket and moved slowly up to the painting. She stared at the eyeball. The eyeball stared right back. She moved to the left. The eyeball followed her. She moved to the right. Once again, the eyeball followed her. Slowly, she reached out and touched the eyeball on the painting.

"Mr. Stubbs," she said. "I think there's something very perplexing going on here." Stubbs was still hiding beneath the blankets.

"Look. Right here, where I cleaned off your muddy paw print. Some of the pigment was removed from the hydrangea flower painting. There must be another painting beneath this one!"

Jesse crawled back into bed and made

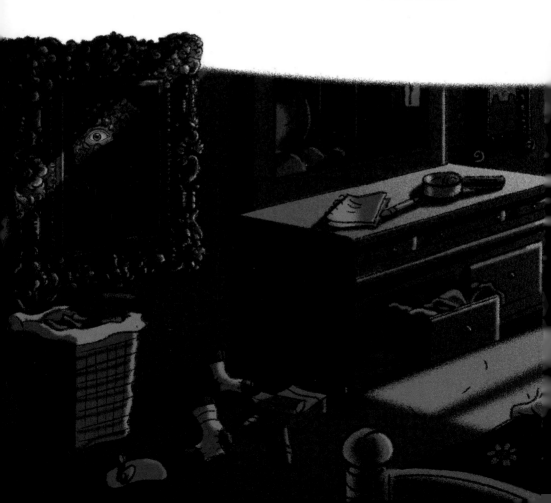

one last entry into her journal for the night:

Sunday morning. 3:00 am.
With Mr. Stubbs' help, I uncovered a
strange, new mystery tonight. But
I'll need some help from Professor
Peach tomorrow to really sort this
puzzle out.

The next morning arrived, and Jesse
finished her daily chores just as fast as she

could and marched next door to The Professor's house. "If anyone can help us figure this one out, it's Professor Peach. After all, he does have advanced degrees in Science, Technology, Engineering, Math, AND ART!" she exclaimed.

"Well, what do we have here, Jesse? It looks like an antique frame and canvas," The Professor questioned Jesse.

"I've got a real puzzler for you this time, Professor." Jesse grinned. She handed the painting of the hydrangea flowers to The Professor.

"Ah-ha! Hydrangea macrophylla," The Professor chimed in.

"Hey! You've been talking to Kimmy Kat Black!" They both laughed.

"So, what is your quandary, my dear?" The Professor asked Jesse with a smile.

"My quandary," Jesse answered, "is this eyeball that I uncovered when I was wiping

Stubbs' paw print off of it. It seems to me that there is another painting beneath this one, and I'm not sure what to do about it."

"Well, let me take a closer look." The Professor held the painting up and studied it carefully with Jesse's magnifying glass. He studied the painting at an angle. He studied it from straight down. He studied it up close, and he studied it from a few steps away. He even scratched it a bit with his fingernail.

"Do you mind if I perform a few tests on your painting, Jesse?" The Professor

asked politely.

"Sure. Knock yourself out." Jesse replied.

"Excuse me?" The Professor asked with a puzzled look.

"I mean, yes. Please go ahead, Professor."

On the front porch of his house, The Professor dipped a small cotton swab in some water and rubbed the painting gently, much like Jesse had done with her bandanna.

"What we have here, Jesse," The Professor informed, "is a water-soluble, tempera painting that was executed on top of a much older painting created in oil paints." He went on, "In my expert opinion, in the field of Art History and the science of fine art restoration, the oil painting below is of far more significance than the more recent, amateur painting of the hydrangea flowers that resides on top."

"So, what do I do?" Jesse asked.

"Well, that's up to you, my dear, but if it

were my painting," The Professor continued, "I would restore it back to its original condition by removing the hydrangea image that occupies the top layer."

With The Professor's guidance, Jesse worked patiently and precisely at restoring the old painting to its original form. Using an entire box of cotton swabs, a full roll of paper towels, and who knows how much water, Jesse slowly removed the painting of

the hydrangea flowers, one small section at a time. Eventually, the entire oil painting that once lay beneath began to reveal itself to the anxious pair. Eyeballs and all!

Jesse lifted the painting so the two could study the results.

"An old portrait painting!" Professor Peach exclaimed. "The dates tell us that this soldier was alive during The Civil War! Jesse, this painting is nearly two hundred years old!" The Professor proclaimed. The Professor was always proclaiming something.

"But who could it be? The only clue here is this cryptic inscription."

P.O.D.

August 4th, 1825

October 15th, 1910

"This is going to require you to do some further research, Jesse, my dear," The Professor said encouragingly.

Birds in the Boneyard

Chapter 7

Jesse jotted the strange inscription down into her journal:

P.O.D.
August 4th, 1825
October 15th, 1910

"Time to make it over to The Deanville Library, Stubbs," she said.

The pair headed straight to the library's reference section and pored through book after book. She read books on Civil War soldiers and looked at dozens and dozens of photographs and illustrations of famous Generals and Colonels. She could not find anything similar to the portrait that she and Professor Peach uncovered.

She looked through art history books at hundreds of portraits from the 18th and 19th centuries. No luck there either.

She searched through dictionaries, almanacs, and encyclopedias for any reference to the mysterious inscription that was on the painting. Nothing.

Jesse even logged on to the library's computer to search the Internet for clues. She spent hours and hours. No luck there either.

"I understand the dates," Jesse said to Stubbs. "The Civil War was from April 12th, 1861, until April 9th, 1865. So, we know the dates are around this time. But what in the world does the phrase 'P.O.D.' mean?"

Frustrated, Jesse packed up her messenger bag to head home. "C'mon, Stubbs. My brain's starting to ache. Let's go home," she said to the cat.

Cutting through the park on the way home, Jesse decided to stop at The Thinkin' Tree.

Jesse climbed up onto the big, low hanging branch of The Thinkin' Tree and dangled there from her knees.

"When I hang upside down, gravity pulls my best ideas down into my brain," she often said as Stubbs looked on.

Jesse thought, *P.O.D... P.O.D... What could that mean? Clark Johnson said it stands for 'Put On Deodorant,' but he's full of baloney.*

Jesse looked up at the sky from her inverted perch and watched as a large congress of ravens flew into The Boneyard—Deanville's old cemetery.

"Hey! Wait one minute!" Jesse whispered to Stubbs as she watched the birds land on the marble headstones. "There are loads of inscriptions on those old grave markers in The Boneyard! There might be a clue over there! C'mon, Stubbs! Let's check it out!"

A Brazen Raven and a Grave Discovery

# Chapter 8

Darkness was beginning to fall on The Boneyard, so Jesse removed her flashlight from her messenger bag. She began to shine it on the markers as she walked slowly through the dark, quiet cemetery.

Bats flittered, moths fluttered, and the wind made howling noises through the branches of the sycamore trees. The moon cast a strange, eerie light upon the cold, marble markers.

"Oh, don't be a scaredy-cat cat," Jesse said to Stubbs, who was huddled behind her leg. "There's nothing to be frightened of here!" Stubbs looked nervous, and Jesse nudged him with her flashlight and laughed.

Suddenly, Jesse heard a strange noise. "Caw! Caw! Caw!"

"Did you hear that, Stubbs?" Jesse asked nervously.

"Caw! Caw! Caw!" She heard it again.

Jesse pointed her flashlight toward the strange sound. "A raven! Look, Stubbs! A huge, black raven!"

Jesse trained the beam of her flashlight on the body of the large, black bird. "Caw!" It squawked again loudly.

Quietly, Jesse moved the flashlight's beam from the bird and slowly down the face of the large, gray tombstone.

The bright beam stopped on a large, chiseled inscription. It read:

Here lies
Colonel Pappy Orvis Dean
The Founder of Deanville
August 4th, 1825
October 15th, 1910

"That's it, Stubbs!" Jesse yelled out.

"P.O.D! Pappy Orvis Dean! The founder of Deanville! That's the answer!" Jesse shouted. "We've done it! We've solved the mystery!"

"Now we have some serious work to do!"

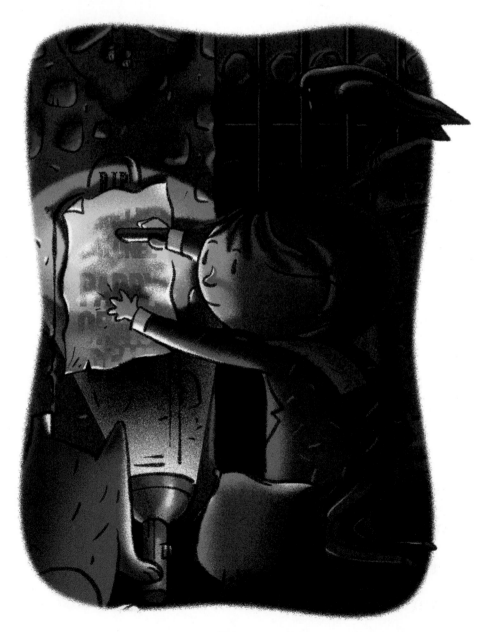

She instructed Stubbs, "Here. Hold my flashlight while I work."

Jesse took blank pages from her journal and a large pencil from her messenger bag. In the light of the moon and from her flashlight, she made an intricate, detailed rubbing of the inscription on the face of the old, marble grave marker.

"There. We've documented our findings, Stubbs," Jesse said as she carefully placed the rubbings into her messenger bag.

"Let's head home, dude! We have some more work to do!"

The next morning, Jesse could not wait to share her findings with Professor Peach.

"Hey Professor! Check these out!" Jesse waved the rubbings from across the lawn.

With Jesse's magnifying glass, Professor Peach studied the rubbing that Jesse had created from the inscription on the old grave marker. "Very interesting," he said slowly.

"Very, very interesting."

The Professor scratched his chin and looked back at Jesse with a smile.

"Jesse, my dear," he said, "with patience, hard work, and persistence, you have made a significant discovery."

"You have unearthed and identified the one and only known image of Colonel Pappy Dean. The founding father of Deanville!" The Professor exclaimed. "The entire town will be proud and grateful!"

"Now, if I only had a way to share this with our community," Jesse said to The Professor.

"Oh, I think I have an idea," Professor Peach said with a wink.

THE END

Colonel Pappy Orvis Dean
The Founder of Deanville
Painting discovered and donated by Jesse Steam
Urban Archaeologist & Restorer of Fine Art

Jesse's Word List

Blathered
talked nonsense—like my algebra teacher

Chiseled
cut—*I chiseled my name in my desk.*

Congress
things in a scary group—like politicians

Cowering
crouching in fear—*I cowered at the algebra test.*

Cryptic
mysterious—*The algebra test was cryptic.*

Flaky
odd—*The flaky lady made flaky pie crust.*

Freaky
strange or weird—like the pie crust lady

Frenzied
excited—*The flaky pie made me frenzied.*

Illuminated
lit up—*His bald head was illuminated.*

Mustered
gathered—*I mustered mustard for the hot dog.*

Patiently
taking your time—like when eating dessert

Patina
the look of something—*He had the patina of rotten wood.*

Peculiar
odd or strange—like your algebra teacher

Perplexing
complicated—like the algebra test

Prehistoric
really, really old—like your algebra teacher

Quandary
perplexed or uncertainty—like when I saw the algebra test

Screeched
the sound I made when I saw the algebra homework

Slumber
sleep—what I want to do in algebra class

Smirk
a smug smile—*I made a smirk when he failed algebra.*

About the Author & Illustrator

Ken Bowser is an illustrator and writer whose work has appeared in hundreds of books and countless periodicals. While he's been drawing for as long as he could hold a pencil, all of his work today is created digitally on a computer. He works out of his home studio in Central Florida with his wife Laura and a big, lazy, orange cat.

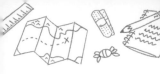

Try It Out!

How to Make a Colorful Crayon Rubbing

In *The Hint in the Peeping Pupil*, Jesse makes a rubbing of an old grave marker in The Boneyard—Deanville's Ancient Cemetery. It's fun and easy to make rubbings with crayons and simple objects!

What You Need: A piece of blank paper. Just about any type of paper will work, but thin paper works the best. Crayons in different colors. Real leaves from your yard or from a park or a forest.

Steps:

1. Collect leaves of various shapes and sizes. You can use fresh leaves or dried fallen leaves.

2. Position a leaf with its bottom side face up.

3. Put a sheet of paper, preferably thin, over the leaf.

4. Rub the side of a crayon gently on the area over the leaf. You'll see the colored areas start to take the shape of the leaf.

5. Continue until you've rubbed over the entire leaf.

6. Remove the leaf to reveal your rubbing!

7. Make more rubbings using other colors and leaf shapes!

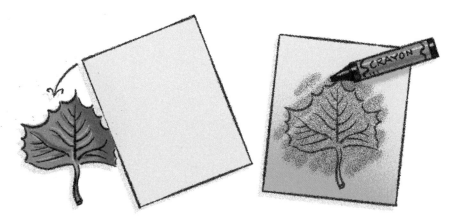